Over many a lifetime,
The legend's been told,
Of a young boy named Maverick,
So adventurous and bold.

On a wilderness journey,
The boy did embark,
To find mythical gemstones,
In Glacier National Park.

He'd heard of sacred pools,
With colors so grand,
Holding promise of things,
He had yet to understand.

With a pep in his step,
And a gleam in his eye,
He ventured forth earnestly,
His trail towards the sky.

Through the towering pine trees,
The aspen and larch,
His spirit came alive,
The further his march.

Passing big lakes and meadows,
And glacier-fed streams,
This mountainous playground,
Only fed his daydreams.

As he rounded the bend,
In a wilderness shire,
A grizzly appeared,
Eyes glowing red like fire.

Maverick started to quake,
When her eyes took aflame,
But they were softened by words,
As she called out his name;

"Maverick, fear not!
You have help from above,
You are safe, you are rooted,
You are grounded in love."

As he journeyed on farther,
On a magical stream,
Swam a harlequin duck,
An orange aura, did gleam.

Swirls of creativity,
As she paddled along,
Maverick heard in his heart,
Her beautiful birdsong;

"You're the Master Creator,
Of your own unique Way,
Create your own music,
Have fun, laugh and play!"

Then up farther still, stood,
On a mountain so sheer,
A mountain goat beaming,
Like the sun, without fear.

The light illuminated,
Maverick's path up the hill,
With confidence to conquer,
This adventurous thrill.

"You'll find treasure up there, Maverick,
But know in your soul,
You're the *most* valued treasure,
You are perfect, and whole."

Maverick paused for a moment,
Pondering what he'd just heard,
And was quite deep in thought,
When a Pika appeared.

A crown on her head sparkled,
With a gemstone so green,
Its heart-shape was flawless,
She looked like a queen.

"In this Universe, Maverick,
(And in the Grand Scheme)
Love is all that is needed,
And Love reigns supreme."

When he rounded the next bend,
As the eagles sung,
A large moose stood tall,
With a sapphire tongue.

Soothing words with such power,
Flowed out from his maw,
The pure strength of his voice,
Left Maverick in awe.

"Speak your truth to the world,
Let your voice be heard!
Maverick, be kind, and be honest,
Be true to your word!"

Then, next on his pathway,
A Bighorn Sheep appeared,
Indigo gem on her forehead,
He noticed, as he neared.

"Be still, just listen, Maverick,
And trust your own gut,
You have intuitive connection,
And you know what is what.

Believe it. And Trust it.
If something's amiss,
Your feelings will guide you,
Always remember this."

Last, on his journey,
Another queen came into sight,
A violet-crowned Lynx,
So regal and bright.

Whispers of the Divine,
Gently danced in the air,
Maverick felt the connection,
With Everyone. Everywhere.

"You are never alone, Child,
You are part of the Whole,
You are Cherished, and Loved,
You are Light, You are Soul."

Maverick's head was spinning,
With insights so grand,
When he rounded the last bend,
The time, now at hand.

He'd come to the moment,
Sacred pools were in view,
Colors swirling, and dancing,
Gemstones in rainbow hue.

He understood everything,
It all made sense now,
As he picked up the gemstones,
He made a sacred vow....

To always remember:

I am safe and protected. To not be afraid.

To be creative, make music, and have fun!

I am treasured, and perfect, and perfectly whole.

To love with all of my heart. Love reigns supreme!

To speak my truth, be kind, be true to my word.

To listen to my intuition, and trust it.

That I'm connected to everyone, everywhere.

And I am LOVED!

Yes,
YOU are LOVED!

Milton Keynes UK
Ingram Content Group UK Ltd.
UKRC030833020424
440455UK00006B/87

9 798210 673886